BY BAXTER BLACK

ILLUSTRATED BY BOB BLACK

Coyote Cowboy Company

Benson, Arizona

2003

Published by: **Coyote Cowboy Company**
P.O. Box 2190
Benson, Arizona 85602
All rights reserved

Illustrated by Bob Black

LIBRARY OF CONGRESS CATALOGING IN PUBLICATION DATA
Main entry under:
Humor-Cowboy

Bibliography: p
1. Humor-Cowboy
2. Agriculture Commentary
3. Comics

I. Black, Baxter Ashby, 1945-

Library of Congress: 2003194713
ISBN: 0-939343-36-3

OTHER BOOKS BY BAXTER

* THE COWBOY AND HIS DOG © 1980
* A RIDER, A ROPER AND A HECK'UVA WINDMILL MAN © 1982
ON THE EDGE OF COMMON SENSE, THE BEST SO FAR © 1983
* DOC, WHILE YER HERE © 1984
BUCKAROO HISTORY © 1985
COYOTE COWBOY POETRY © 1986
✓CROUTONS ON A COW PIE © 1988
✓THE BUCKSKIN MARE © 1989
✓COWBOY STANDARD TIME © 1990
CROUTONS ON A COW PIE, VOL 2 © 1992
HEY, COWBOY, WANNA GET LUCKY? © 1994
(*Crown Publishing, Inc.*)
✗DUNNY AND THE DUCK © 1994
✗COW ATTACK © 1996
CACTUS TRACKS AND COWBOY PHILOSOPHY © 1997
(*Crown Publishing, Inc.*)
✗LOOSE COW PARTY © 1998
A COWFUL OF COWBOY POETRY © 2000
HORSESHOES, COWSOCKS & DUCKFEET © 2003
(*Crown Publishing, Inc.*)

* included in Coyote Cowboy Poetry - 1986
✓included in Croutons On a Cow Pie, Vol 2 - 1992
✗included in A Cowful of Cowboy Poetry - 2000

Our special thanks from the crew at Coyote Cowboy Company to Carolyn Nolting and Jennifer and Will Cubbage for their significant contribution.

Brother Bob and I would like to dedicate this book to ag kids across the country who understand the value of labor, the secret world of animals and the love of the land. And especially to our ag teacher, Rupert Mansell who helped show us the way, and to our mother who raised us right.

WITHDRAWN

INTRODUCTION

Many of us who make our living in agriculture have watched our children over the years come home from town or school with, for lack of a better word, propaganda. Ideas, pamphlets, work projects, posters or assignments that paint those of us who make a living off the land as villains, or at least, as prehistoric.

It is frustrating. We have to explain to our kids that there are people who make a living trying to convince urban consumers that modern agriculture is bad. They are against any or all combinations of cows, breaking ground, eating meat, chemical fertilizer, feedlots, genetically modified foods, antibiotics, grazing, growth promotants, farm subsidies, herbicides, predator control, food for profit and productive use of public lands.

They, the ANTI's I call them, take for granted that we have the safest, cheapest and most plentiful food supply on earth. They choose to ignore that it is us that the world turns to when they can't feed themselves. And they never question where their own next meal will come from.

Ag Man rose from the depths of my brain to battle the enemies of agriculture. Brother Bob brought him to life. Suitable for young people, written at an adult level, our super hero takes on the ANTI's and in the process, examines many issues that confront modern agriculture including animal rights, confinement feeding, genetic manipulation, endangered species relocation, urban encroachment, bioterrorism, market manipulation, vandalism, disease, pestilence and armadillo mutants.

This is not a deep tome, but it was fun to write and I got if off my chest. I hope it is fun to read.

baxter

P.S. At the risk of making this book educational, a teacher's guide is available. It consists of 12-15 multiple choice questions for each storyline pertinent to the particular subject. It includes referenced answer sheets. It is designed to be a guide for discussion. Call the Coyote Cowboy Company at (800) 654-2550 for information.

TABLE OF CONTENTS

Our Main Characters

Corn Silk - Ag reporter, multi-media, sharp, articulate, knowledgeable, independent . . . the daring distaff.

Farm Boy - Typical teenage farm kid . . . computer literate, machinery obsessed and agriculturally cognitive. Cool.

Ag Man - Super Hero - can transform into anything mechanical (combine, Shop Vac, sphygmomanometer) with just the twist of his cap. Sincere, powerful and always on the side of right.

LOCUST PLAGUE

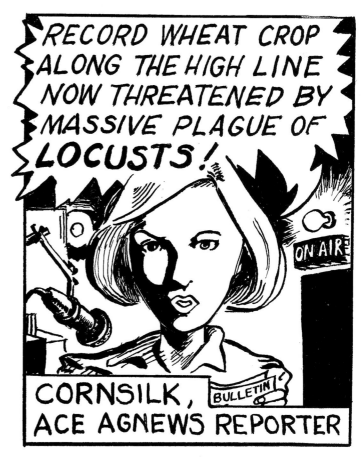

A RUTHLESS ARMY OF LOCUSTS IS SWEEPING THROUGH NORT COUNTY AT TWO MILES A DAY...

WHEAT FARMERS ARE DESPERATELY COMBINING TO STAY AHEAD OF THE PLAGUE.

ONLY ONE BIG WHEAT FARM REMAINS IN THE PATH OF THE VORACIOUS LOCUSTS!

THAT'S US, DAD... WHEN WILL THE COMBINE CREW GET HERE?

SOON, DARLIN'

I HOPE

AG MAN! A WHEAT FARMER IN NORT COUNTY IS IN THE LOCUST'S PATH! HIS CROP LOOKS DOOMED!

ROGER, CORNSILK! THANKS

FARMBOY! GRAB YOUR ENTOMOLOGY BOOK, LET'S SEE IF WE CAN HELP!

WHOA

WITH A TWIST OF HIS CAP AG MAN TRANSFORMS HIMSELF INTO AN F3 TORNADO

ALWAYS BUCKLE UP, FARMBOY.

WOOOOOOSH

GREAT GOBBLING GRAIN, AG MAN! I HOPE WE'RE NOT TOO LATE!

MR. McRAE! HAS THE COMBINE CREW ARRIVED?

AG MAN!

THEY JUST GOT HERE! I SENT THEM TO START ON THE EAST SIDE. C'MON, LET'S CHECK 'EM OUT!

FARMBOY!?

WHOMP!

LOOK! THEY'RE ALREADY MOVING FOUR ABREAST!

AG MAN...

AG MAN! SAVE US!

FEAR NOT LITTLE NELL.

WITH A TWIST OF HIS CAP, AG MAN TRANSFORMS HIS HEAD INTO A G.E. TURBOJET!

K-FOOMP!

I'LL INCINERATE 'EM!

IT'S NOT WORKING, FARMBOY... BUT WAIT! I'VE GOT ANOTHER IDEA!

WHAT NOW?

AG MAN, IN A *HEROIC* ATTEMPT TO STOP THE LOCUSTS, TRANSFORMS

shop·vac 175 million gallon

... INTO A GIANT *SHOP·VAC!*

SLURP

SHUT IT DOWN!

THEY'VE PLUGGED YOUR FILTER! YOU'RE ON FIRE!

K·BOOM

POP SIZZLE

HANG ON, AG MAN!

A TWIST OF THE CAP RETURNS SHOP VAC BACK INTO AG MAN.

PITOOOOEE

PUSH

AG MAN RECOVERS BUT THE SKIES ARE STILL *GREEN* WITH *MENACE.*

PTTTT

I'M OK NOW, FARMBOY. YOU SAVED MY LIFE. ANY INFORMATION IN THE *BUG BOOK?*

ROGER THAT! BUGS COMMUNICATE CHEMICALLY BY SECRETING TINY LEVELS OF *PHEROMONES* WHICH OTHER INSECTS OF THE SAME SPECIES CAN DETECT *MILES AWAY!*

SO... IF WE HAD SOME OF THIS STUFF... THE LOCUSTS WOULD... *FOLLOW US?*

BUGS

AWAY FROM *THE FARM!*

LIKE THE *PIED PIPER!*

CAN WE *GET* IT??

HERE, CALL CORNSILK! SHE CAN RUSH SOME FROM THE *UNIVERSITY*

BLIP

HERE'S THE LOCUST PHEROMONES! THE PROFESSOR SAYS THEY'RE *POTENT!*

SOON

A SOAKED *CLOTH* WILL SPREAD THE *FUMES!* FARMBOY, GIVE ME YOUR SHIRT!

BUT... AG MAN, THIS IS MY AUTOGRAPHED *FARM-AID T-SHIRT!*

FARM·AID

FOR THE SAKE OF AGRICULTURE AS WE KNOW IT... *PLEASE.*

GOOD LAD, THANKS

MY SHIRT

AND *NOW...*

Locust Plague

HOG FARM DISASTER

Hog Farm Disaster

WE'RE ALL WORRIED ABOUT THE IMPACT OF *MONOLITHIC HOG FARMS* ON THE COMMUNITY.

THE SMELL? THE MARKET EFFECT? THE INFLUENCE ON LOCAL POLITICIANS?

PERSONALLY, I'M WILLING TO GIVE THEM A CHANCE...

BUT NOW *THIS*...

AG MAN, TRANSFORMED INTO A *FOUR WHEELER*, ARRIVES WITH FARMBOY AT THE WHEEL.

VRRROOOMM

LET'S GET TO WORK, FARM BOY!

SKRAAAAAAAAK

SLURP

MOVING AT SUPERPOWER SPEED AG MAN TRANSFORMS FROM ATV-TO BULLDOZER-TO HONEYWAGON...

AND FINALLY HE TRANSFORMS INTO A 650 GANG DISK.

HOLY HAM HOCKS, AG MAN! THAT SURE LOOKS *AND* SMELLS BETTER!

YES, FARM BOY, BUT I'M WORRIED IT WAS *NOT* AN ACCIDENT.

I MANAGE THIS HOG FARM, AG MAN, AND I'VE JUST RECEIVED THIS *FAX* FROM *L.E.T.O.Ps.*!

LUNATICS FOR ETHICAL TREATMENT OF PIGS.

THEY ARE *DEMANDING* WE SET ALL THE PIGS *FREE!*

MGR

AGRIZAM! THIRTY THOUSAND PIGS LOOSE ON THE HIGHWAY!

YES, AG MAN, *OR...*

else... We Will BOMB ANOTHER HOG FARM TONIGHT

L.E.T.O.P.

MEANWHILE, AT THE SECRET HEADQUARTERS OF *L.E.T.O.Ps.* ~LUNATICS FOR ETHICAL TREATMENT OF PIGS ~

WE DID IT, MADAM FELDA.

DUMPED THIRTY MILLION GALLONS OF HOG WASTE ON THE COMMUNITY.

WELL DONE BOYS. THIS SHOULD STIMULATE DONATIONS TO OUR CAUSE.

THIS EVENING THE WASTE LAGOON AT GIANT HOG FARMS IN PANTOWN WILL FEEL *L.E.T.O.Ps.* STING!

OINK OINK OINK OINK OINK OINK OINK OINK OINK

AND I DO HOPE THAT *SHOAT FACE, AG MAN,* SHOWS UP. HE'LL GET HIS *PIG'S FEET PICKLED!*

Hog Farm Disaster

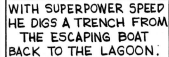

WITH A TWIST OF HIS CAP AG MAN TRANSFORMS HIMSELF INTO A MODEL R 100 DITCH WITCH!

TO THE LAGOON, FARMBOY!

ROAR

WITH SUPERPOWER SPEED HE DIGS A TRENCH FROM THE ESCAPING BOAT BACK TO THE LAGOON.

ESCAPING BOAT

TRENCHER'S PATH

THE HOG WASTE RIVER REVERSES ITS FLOW.

WE'RE BEING SUCKED BACK TO THE LAGOON, YOU IDIOTS! DO SOMETHING!

ROW!

BUT... BUT... IT'S A MOTORBOAT

AG MAN TRANSFORMS INTO A MONSTER COAL SHOVEL

CHOMP

IN FIVE MINUTES HE DEEPENS THE WASTE LAGOON BY TEN FEET.

NOOOOOO! WE'RE BACK IN THE LAGOON!

PLOP!

WITH ONE SCOOP THE DAM IS CLOSED AND THE VILLAINS CAUGHT.

HEY! THE SABOTEURS ARE MAKING FOR THE FAR BANK!

LET'S SEE HOW THEY LIKE MY HARPOON ARM

BING

AG MAN HARPOON COMPANY

WITH AN EXPLOSIVE WARHEAD! COOL! SHOOT FROM THE HIP, AG MAN!

NO, NO, FARMBOY, NEVER HAVE FUN WITH FIREARMS

BLAM

OOPS

BOOM

MADAM FELDA, THE LUNATICS FOR ETHICAL TREATMENT OF PIGS HAVE SABOTAGED THEIR LAST HOG FARM

WE CAN'T THANK YOU ENOUGH, AG MAN. WE'LL FINISH CLEANING UP THIS MESS RIGHT AWAY.

YES, AND KEEP IT THAT WAY. BIG AGRIBUSINESS HAS A RESPONSIBILITY TO ITS NEIGHBORS.

AND LOOK WHO'S HELPING WITH THE CLEANUP. I THINK MADAM FELDA AND HER HENCHMEN HAVE LEARNED A LESSON.

DON'T YOU MEAN STENCHMEN.

HA HA, YOU'RE VERY HUMOROUS, FARMBOY.

MAILBOX VANDALS

A WEEK LATER, IN TOWN

WHATCHA WANNA DO TONIGHT, SHARKY?

I SAY WE BASH SOME BOXES ON CO-OP ROAD.

BUT... WE DID THOSE LAST WEEK.

YEAH! SO THEY'LL ALL HAVE NEW BOXES! HEEEAH!

... AT THE GRANGE HALL THE FIRST BOX IS ROBERTS'. WE GUARD IT EVERY NIGHT. WHEN THEY START, WE CALL EVERYONE AND MEET AT MY HOUSE TO SET THE TRAP!

SO WE'VE GOT A PLAN.

IS THIS LEGAL?

IS BOX BASHIN'?!

AG MAN! VIGILANTES ARE SET TO AMBUSH THOSE MAILBOX VANDALS IN JONESVILLE. SOUNDS LIKE TROUBLE!

CORNSILK OF THE AGNEWS

THANKS, CORNSILK! I'D BETTER TALK TO THEM BEFORE THEY DO SOMETHING THEY'LL REGRET!

MAILBOX VANDALISM IS LOWER THAN KICKING DOGS, BESIDES BEING A FEDERAL OFFENSE!

COME, FARMBOY! WE'RE OFF TO JONESVILLE TO DELIVER THE MAIL!

I UNDERSTAND YOUR ANGER HOWARD, BUT PLEASE GIVE THE LAW A CHANCE.

NO! IT'S TOO LATE FOR THAT, AG MAN!

HE WON'T TELL US THEIR PLANS. ALL WE CAN DO IS WAIT, FARMBOY... FARMBOY!

DEEP IN THE NIGHT ON CO-OP ROAD...

ARE YOU READY, SHARKY?

VRUMMM VRUMMM

READY, BOBO... HEY, MUSTN'T FORGET MY SAFETY GOGGLES! HEEHEHEHE

ONE-INCH IRON PIPE

WELDING GLOVES

ELECTRICAL TAPE

THE VANDALS HIT ROBERTS' MAILBOX AND...

WHAP!

THE VIGILANTES' PLAN SWINGS INTO ACTION

THEY TOOK OUT ROBERTS' BOX AND NEARLY GOT ME WITH IT!

BUT UNBEKNOWNST TO ALL AG MAN WAITS DOWNROAD.

HOLD UP BOYS! LET'S TALK A MINUTE!

WHUMP

WHOA! I THINK WE HIT A COW!

EEEEEEEEE

THE VANDALS HAVE RUN DOWN AG MAN IN THE ROAD

THAT WAS NO COW! THAT WAS MY SISTER! HE HEEEHE

BUT WAITING JUST AHEAD, THE VIGILANTE'S HAVE SET THEIR TRAP!

PLYWOOD SHEET FULL OF NAILS!

BATTERY WIRE TO EXPLOSIVE CHARGE!

I STUFFED THE BOX WITH DIRTY CHICKEN FEATHERS TOO!

I HEAR 'EM!

OLD 2% MILK

DAY-GLO PINK ENAMEL

GUN POWDER

U.S. MAIL

LOOKS LIKE A RIPE ONE, SHARKY!

BATTERRRRUP!

KA-BOOM!

THE MAILBOX VANDALS HAVE HIT THE BOOBY-TRAPPED MAILBOX.

FLIP CRUNCH

LOOK! WE'RE TOO LATE, FARMBOY! LET'S HOPE NO ONE'S HURT!

WHAT'S HAPPENED!? THIS ONE'S OUT COLD... HEY! THE OTHER ONE'S RUNNIN', GET 'EM BOYS!

FARMBOY! ADMINISTER AID TO THE DRIVER! I'LL FOLLOW THE MOB!

CHECK!

THERE HE IS! BY THE TRACKS! HEADED FOR THE GRAIN ELEVATOR!

GIT 'EM!

THE FOOL'S GOIN' UP! WE GOT HIM NOW!

HE'LL BE SORRY HE PICKED ON OUR MAILBOXES!

HOLD UP, MEN! PLEASE. LET ME TRY TO TALK HIM DOWN.

WITH A TWIST OF HIS HAT AG MAN TRANSFORMS HIS HANDS AND FEET INTO ELECTROMAGNETS AND CLIMBS THE ELEVATOR.

CLANG CLANG CLANG CLANG

SO THEY SENT THE HUMAN COCKROACH.

THERE'S NO EXCUSE FOR WANTON DESTRUCTION OF OTHERS' PROPERTY BUT IF YOU SURRENDER AND APOLOGIZE, I'LL TRY AND REASON WITH THE MOB.

HOW'S THIS FOR REASON FLANGE FOOT!

HOLD STILL!!

IT LOOKS LIKE AG MAN IS HOLDING BACK.

YOU'RE JUST A TEENAGER, SON. GIVE IT UP BEFORE YOU SCAR YOUR LIFE FOREVER.

PLUCK

LEGGO MY ARM!

OH NO!

SHARKY JERKS BACK AND GOES OVER THE RAIL.

HANG ON KID!

YEAH! AN USE YER THUMB! YER NOT DRIVIN' A TRACTOR, Y'KNOW!

AS SHARKY FALLS AG MAN TWISTS HIS HAT AND TRANSFORMS HIS ARM INTO A GIANT ROLL OF *CHICKEN WIRE!*

HELP!

AAAYYYYYEEEE ZZING

AG MAN SNAGS SHARKY A MERE TEN FEET OFF THE GROUND!

FOOMP!

ALRIGHT, MEN, I'LL LOWER HIM DOWN IF YOU'LL AGREE TO LET THE *LAW* HANDLE THIS.

MAYBE AG MAN'S RIGHT!

I DUNNO, I'D SURE LIKE TO *HORSEWHIP* THOSE *VANDALS!*

THEY'VE ALREADY BEEN *PAINTED, FEATHERED* AND *BLOWN SKY HIGH.*

YOU WIN, AG MAN. WE AGREE! IT'S IN THE LAW'S HANDS NOW!

YOU DID THE RIGHT THING, HOWARD.

YOU'RE RIGHT, AG MAN. VIGILANTISM IS WRONG...

...IT'S JUST SO... FRUSTRATING!

MAILBOX VANDALISM IS A SERIOUS CRIME AND THEY'LL BE PUNISHED ACCORDINGLY.

BUT THEY'RE JUST BOYS. LET'S HOPE THEY GROW INTO BETTER MEN.

C'MON, FARMBOY, IT'S STARTING TO RAIN.

THROUGH RAIN OR SLEET OR VANDALS OR HAIL, *AG MAN* WILL HELP DELIVER *THE MAIL!*

THAT'S VERY GOOD, FARMBOY.

IS THAT ORIGINAL?

THE MAD COW SMUGGLERS

A PHONE RINGS ON A DAIRY BACK EAST...

BILL, SOMETHIN' AWFUL'S HAPPENED HERE AND THE OFFICALS *WON'T LISTEN!*

I SAW HEAD SUFFERIN' FROM *MAD COW* BEING LOADED ON A SHIP FOR AMERICA!

WELL DONE, NIGEL. I KNOW JUST WHO TO CALL!

YES, CORNSILK! I GOT THE NEWS FROM MY COUSIN IN ENGLAND!

THIS IS A JOB FOR AG MAN!

THANKS CORNSILK, WE'LL HAVE TO MOVE *FAST!* IT SOUNDS LIKE THE *ANTI'S* ARE *ON THE WARPATH!*

ANTI'S?

FARMBOY! THE ANTI'S [ACTIVISTS AGAINST NEARLY EVERYTING] ARE TRYING TO SMUGGLE *MAD COWS* INTO THE COUNTRY!

OH NO!

...WHILE ON A SHIP NEAR THE EASTERN SEABOARD

IT'S THE *PERFECT PLAN*, LYMON, THE *PUBLIC* WILL PANIC!

YES! THE *DAIRY* AND *BEEF* INDUSTRIES WILL *COLLAPSE* AND COWS WILL BE *FREE!*

FREE COWS! HEY! I COULD START MY *OWN* DAIRY!

CORNSILK, WHAT HAVE YOU FOUND?

WE KNOW THE ANTI'S LEFT BRITAIN EIGHT DAYS AGO IN A *REFITTED TRAWLER!*

SO!

THEY COULD ALMOST BE HERE!

AGRAZAM, AG MAN. WE'VE GOT TO *LOCATE* THAT SHIP BEFORE THEY REACH THE COAST!

YOU BET YOUR BRAIN STEM, FARM BOY, LET'S MOBILIZE!

I'LL TRACK YOU ON THE AG-SAT!

TO LOCATE THE *MAD COW* SMUGGLER'S SHIP, AG MAN *TRANSFORMS* INTO A *RECONNAISSANCE SATELLITE* HIGH ABOVE THE ATLANTIC OCEAN.

WOW, AG MAN! THESE DIGITAL PICTURES ARE GREAT!

KEEP YOUR EYES PEELED, FARM BOY.

CORNSILK MONITORS THE BOYS FROM HER MOBILE SPACE LINK.

AG MAN, I SEE 'EM!

NO, FARM BOY, IT'S JUST A POD OF MIGRATING HUMPBACKS. *KEEP LOOKING. WAIT!* I SEE GEORGE STRAIT'S BUS!

AG MAN, TRANSFORMED INTO A RE-CON SATELLITE, SCANS THE ATLANTIC FOR THE SHIP THAT IS SMUGGLING *MAD COWS.*

THERE! DOCKING IN COASTVILLE!

THAT'S CLOSE, I'LL GET HELP AND *MEET* YOU THERE!

VRROOM

WITH A TWIST OF HIS CAP, AG MAN TRANSFORMS INTO AN *APOLLO COMMAND MODULE.*

TAKE HER TO WARP THREE FARMEY!

FER CRYIN' OUT LOUD, EGG MON! I'M GIVIN' 'ER ALL SHE'S GOT!

AG MAN AND FARM BOY TOUCHDOWN ON THE DECK OF THE ANTI'S SHIP...

WELL, BLESS MY BONES! IF IT ISN'T THE *EVER-VIGILANT* BAG MAN.

YES, LYMON! AND IF YOU THINK I WON'T SPAR WITH A MAN WHO WEARS EARMUFFS... THINK AGAIN!

GRRRRRRR

EARM...?! YOU IDIOT! THESE ARE *MAD COW* TRANSLATORS! SIC 'EM BOSSIES!

BUT... AGRIZAM! I *CAN'T* STRIKE AN UNHORNED COW!

HA!

UNDER LYMON'S ORDERS, THE *MAD COWS* PIN AG MAN *TO THE DECK.*

AHH, SAMSON, NO CAP, NO POWER. THAT HOW IT WORKS?

SUDDENLY, FROM THE HOLD, FARM BOY IMITATES A BAWLING CALF.

MMMBWAAAAAA

AAAH

YOU *FOOLS!* IT'S A TRICK!

MMMOOO MMMO MOOO MMM MOOO

GET HIM!

ER... AYE, AYE, SIR

THE *ANTI'S LOCK HORNS WITH AG MAN AND FARM BOY.

CAREFUL, AG MAN, COWPIE AT TEN O'CLOCK!

OOF

AAH

*ACTIVISTS AGAINST NEARLY EVERYTING

HELP ARRIVES.

CORNSILK! WATCH THE DECK, IT'S SLIPPERY!

3-2

WELL, I'M NOT *SURPRISED,* IT'S THE *POOP DECK.*

AG MAN, TRANSFORMED INTO A SQUEEZE CHUTE, CORRALS THE ANTI'S SO THEY CAN BE HANDCUFFED BY THE AUTHORITIES.

HEY! WHAT ABOUT OUR RIGHTS!

YES, YOU HAVE RIGHTS. AMONG THEM THE RIGHT TO REMAIN STUPID. BOOK 'EM ON A 102, OFFICER, COW-NAPPING!

THAT WAS A CLOSE CALL, AG MAN!

YES, FARM BOY, AS LONG AS MANIACS LIKE LYMON...

HOLY COW! WHERE'S LYMON!

LYMON, LEADER OF THE ANIMAL RIGHTS TERRORISTS, IS ESCAPING.

THERE HE GOES!

WITH A TWIST OF HIS CAP, AG MAN TRANSFORMS INTO A JET SKI.

LIFE JACKET, FARM BOY?

WHOA, CORNSILK! CARVE IT OUT!

OH GREAT! I'M BEING CHASED BY A WOMAN DRIVER, A TEEN MUTANT AND A TALKING BOAT!

AG MAN, AS A JET SKI, CATCHES THE EVIL LYMON AND CIRCLES HIM AT 238 KNOTS...

...CREATING A WHIRLPOOL!

TIME TO CULL OUT ANOTHER CHRONIC MISCREANT.

IT'S JAIL FOR YOU, LYMON. YOUR INHUMANE PLAN IS FOILED.

SAY CHEESE!

AG MAN, FARM BOY, CORNSILK...WE CAN'T THANK YOU ENOUGH!

YOU'RE WELCOME. WANTON ACTS OF TERRORISM AGAINST AGRICULTURE, EVEN IN THE NAME OF ANIMAL RIGHTS, MUST NOT BE TOLERATED! WE MUST ALL BE ON GUARD.

CALL ME A CAB, FARM BOY... AND WE'LL BE OFF.

YER A CAB

PING!

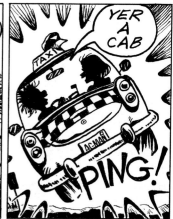

ARMADILLO MUTANTS

YES, AND THE COUNTY AGENT SAYS *HOLES* ARE *APPEARING* IN THE GOLF COURSE.

DIVOTS?

ONLY IF THE JOLLY GREEN GIANT PLAYS GOLF.

WHUMP!

LOOK OUT!

AG MAN HAS HIT SOME-THING ON THE HIGHWAY.

WHOA! *"STEGOSAURUS OVERSLEEPS, WAKES UP IN AGE OF MAMMALS, FILM AT ELEVEN!"*

AFTER CALLING HIGHWAY MAINTENANCE TO REMOVE THE STRANGE CARCASS, AG MAN QUESTIONS THE GOLF PRO ABOUT THE HOLES.

"HOW DEEP ARE THEY?" YOU *THINK* I'D GO *IN?!* HEY, I'M NO LUNKHEAD!

AG MAN TRANSFORMS HIS FIST INTO A LAMP WITH A TWIST OF HIS CAP.

OK, I GUESS IT'S UP TO US.

LET'S STICK TOGETHER

DOES THIS MAKE US SPELUNKHEADS?

AYEEE!

A *MUTANT ARMADILLO!*

RUN FOR YOUR LIVES

DUCKING THE SLASHING CLAWS, AG MAN FINDS HIMSELF THROWN TO THE GROUND.

...HIS DESPERATE STRUGGLE SEEMS LOST WHEN SUDDENLY...

CORNSILK TWISTS HIS CAP, TRANSFORMING HIM INTO THE ARMADILLO'S NATURAL ENEMY...

YOU'RE PROBABLY RIGHT ...BUT STAY TUNED.

TRAPPED IN THE ARMADILLO'S DEN, *AG MAN TRANSFORMS* INTO A 66x43x25 FIRESTONE MUD TIRE SPINNING AT SIXTY MPH.

RRRRR

EEP!

SCREECH VROOM WHAP

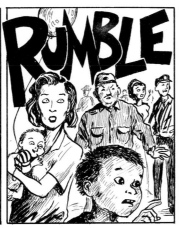

CORNSILK, FARM BOY! SEE IF YOU CAN HERD THE ARMADILLOS ONTO THE TRACK WHILE I...

LAST PLACE
PEACHES
SIN AGUA COUN...

AG MAN, YOU'RE NOT GOING TO EAT.. THAT.. EEEUUGHHHH...

CHOMP GNAW CHEW BURP

WHILE AG MAN GOBBLES, FARM BOY, CORNSILK AND HELPERS BEGAN DRIVING THE SIX ARMADILLOS TOWARD THE TRACK.

AN *ARMADILLO DRIVE?!* IT'S NOT ON THE PROGRAM.

AG MAN, WITH HELP, MANAGES TO HERD THE GIANT MUTANT ARMADILLOS ON TO THE FAIRGROUNDS RACE TRACK.

HE RACES AHEAD AND WITH A TWIST OF HIS CAP..

TRANSFORMS INTO A GIANT SHEET OF ARMADILLO PAPER, SMELLING FAINTLY OF ROTTING FRUIT.

WOOOOSH

AG MAN, TRANSFORMED INTO A STICKY SHEET OF ARMADILLO PAPER LAYS ACROSS THE TRACK

RUMBLE

DRAWN TO THE SCENT OF ROTTING FRUIT, THE GIANT MUTANT ARMADILLOS CHARGE ONTO THE TRAP.

CRASH

WHAT *IS* THAT SMELL?

IT WASN'T ME.

VRUMMMMMM

THANKS, AG MAN, CORNSILK, FARM BOY.

YOU'RE WELCOME, CARLOS. BUT YOUR KNOWLEDGE OF THEIR BEHAVIOR WAS INVALUABLE

COUNTY AGENT

WHAT WILL HAPPEN TO THE MUTANT ARMADILLOS?

I THINK THE PROFESSOR HAS A PLAN...

PROF. BILL'S WILD WEST **TRADING POST** SEE LIVE RATTLERS! *SEE* IF YOU DARE! THE FEROCIOUS **ARMADILLO REX!**

JEWLERY MOCCASINS

I WON'T SELL! THIS FARM'S BEEN IN *MY FAMILY* FOR *THREE GENERATIONS!*

YOU CAN'T STOP *PROGRESS!* *LOOK!*

KUDZU
KATASTROPHE

FARMIN' IS SO *RISKY...* I'LL MAKE YOU *RICH!*

I DON'T NEED YOUR MONEY, SLICK. WHEN THIS SOYBEAN CROP COMES IN I CAN PAY OFF MY LOAN.

WHAT ARE WE DOIN' BOSS?

SLICK REALTY 555-7803

CHUFF CHUFF CHUFF

WE'RE SEEDING HIS SOYBEAN FIELDS WITH PUERARIA TYRANUS... KUDZU 2!

IN TWO WEEKS IT WILL WIPE OUT HIS CROP!

AND...HE'LL BE FORCED TO SELL THE FARM! HA HA HA!

I DON'T UNDERSTAND, AG MAN, THE KUDZU HAS OVER RUN MY SOYBEAN FIELDS.

BUT NOTHING ELSE?

IT'S ALMOST LIKE IT WAS PLANTED.

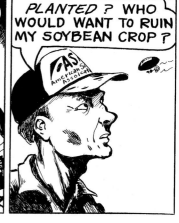

PLANTED? WHO WOULD WANT TO RUIN MY SOYBEAN CROP?

LOOKS LIKE WE MISSED A SPOT, BRUNO.

KUDZU 2

BUT...BOSS, THIS IS THE FAMILY CEMETARY.

GREAT! A LITTLE CALCIUM MIGHT HELP IT GROW! HA HA HA!

CHUFF CHUFF CHUFF

DOES THAT LOOK SUSPICIOUS TO YOU FARM BOY?

WITH A TWIST OF HIS CAP, AG MAN TRANSFORMS INTO A HOVERCRAFT. FARM BOY TAKES THE HELM.

JUMP ON!

WRRRR

THEY FLY TOWARD THE CEMETARY.

ZOOM

DUMP ALL THE SEED, BRUNO!

KUDZU SEEDS

AHHCHOO!

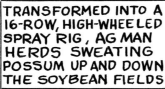

HEAD TOWARD THE WOODS, BRUNO.

THAT DEVIOUS SLICK HAS KIDNAPPED THE POSSUMS!

AG MAN TRANSFORMS HIS FEET INTO OFF-ROAD ROCKET-POWERED ROLLER BLADES.

AEEEYA ZOOM

BLAM!

AG MAN, LOOK OUT! HE'S GOT A LOG!

GRRRRR

TAKE THAT! FLIP

OK, BUT I NORMALLY GIVE ESTIMATES BEFORE I DO ANY FINISH WORK

WHAM GRIND

THE AG MAN WOOD CHIPPER JR.

BRUNO COMES FROM BEHIND

OOPS

OLE! TORO!

OOF!

THE SHIFTY SLICK FALLS, SMASHING THE MUSK VIAL

EHHH, I'M DRIPPING WITH MUSK.

HUMMM... SOAKED IN POSSUM MUSK HEY?

YES, THIS IS A MUCH BETTER WAY.

THANKS, AG MAN. THE KUDZU IS CONTROLLED, MY SOYBEAN CROP WILL PAY THE LOAN AND...

ASA American Soybean Association

MY FARM WON'T BECOME ANOTHER SUBDIVISION.

CHUFF CHUFF

IN THE REPAIRED BALLOON.

FARM BOY, CORNSILK. A LITTLE TO THE EAST.

FEEDLOT FIASCO

Feedlot Fiasco

THANKS FOR COMING DOWN TO THE FEEDYARD, AG MAN.

MALDIVA'S EXPOSÉ ON LOCATION CHannel 17 cool TV

MY HAIR, LOR, DARLING?

BEAUTIFUL, BABY, BEAUTIFUL!

FEEDLOT SCRIPT!

THIS WEEK ON MALDIVA'S EXPOSÉ, THE FEEDLOT'S DIRTY SECRET...

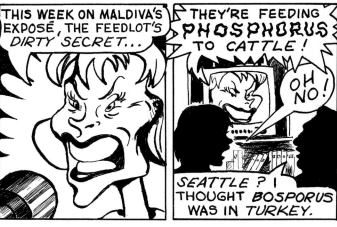

THEY'RE FEEDING PHOSPHORUS TO CATTLE!

OH NO!

SEATTLE? I THOUGHT BOSPORUS WAS IN TURKEY.

OF COURSE WE SUPPLEMENT PHOSPHORUS TO CATTLE, SO WHAT?

WELL, DUH!

PHOSPHORUS IS A CHEMICAL! IT HAS AN ATOMIC NUMBER! AND WE ALL KNOW WHAT THAT MEANS!

YES, BUT...

LOOK OUT!

HERE THEY COME

THE INEVITABLE MEDIA INVASION.

MALDIVA'S EXPOSÉ INCITES A MEDIA ONSLAUGHT.

THEY'VE STAMPEDED THE CATTLE! THEY'RE HEADING FOR THE SCHOOLYARD!

AG MAN TRANSFORMS INTO THE NARWHAL MOBILE SORT OF A CETACEAN 4×4.

LOOK! THOSE KIDS ARE GONNA GET TRAMPLED!

REACHING THE SCHOOL-YARD AHEAD OF THE STAMPEDING CATTLE, AG MAN TRANSFORMS

INTO THE BOW OF THE TITANIC! THE KIDS HUNKER BEHIND HIM.

HOLD STILL, STEER!

CHANNEL 40 eyeball News

I HEAR YOU COWS ARE RUMINANTS, DOES THAT MEAN YOU TALK BEHIND EACH OTHER'S BACK?

GET IT? RUMORS?

THE MEDIA INVASION HAS CAUSED THE STEERS TO ESCAPE.

HOW CAN WE GET THEM BACK TO THE FEEDLOT?

ANY IDEAS, FARMBOY?

WWW. COWPANIC.COM

CATTLE HAVE AN INSTINCTIVE FEAR OF THE BUZZING OF THE *HEEL FLY*, *Hypoderma lineatum!*

BUT, I CAN'T TRANSFORM INTO *ANIMALS*.

NO PROBLEMA

WHAT HAS FARMBOY'S NIMBLE CEREBRUM THOUGHT UP NOW?

AS A MOTOR, WE COULD PROGRAM YOU TO SOUND LIKE THE *HEEL FLY*

BINGO! AND FRIGHTEN THE CRITTERS BACK TO THE FEEDLOT!

WHAT KIND OF MOTOR?

NOSE HAIR CLIPPER? CHAIN SAW? CUMMINS TURBO DIESEL?

WEED EATER! THIRTY CCs, GAS!

WWW. HARMONIC FREQUENCIES.COM

HEEL FLYS MUSICAL EQU WEED EATERS

I THINK WE'RE GRASPING AT WEEDS HERE, FARMBOY.

CHOKE IT, AG MAN! CHOKE IT!

AG MAN HAS TRANSFORMED INTO A WEED EATER THAT MIMICS THE BUZZING OF THE HEEL FLY.

ZZZZZZZ

THEY'RE OFF AND GADDING!

HERE COME THOSE STUPID COWS AND THEY'RE GOING TO GET DUST ALL OVER ME!

LOOK! IT'S MALDIVA! SHE'LL BE CRUSHED IN THE STAMPEDE!

WHO WILL SAVE HER? ...WELL, DUH.

AG MAN LEAPS TO THE BACKS OF THE STAMPEDING CATTLE.

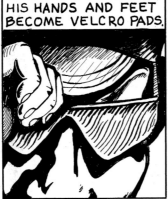

WITH A TWIST OF HIS CAP, HIS HANDS AND FEET BECOME VELCRO PADS.

ENABLING HIM TO RUN OVER THE TOP OF THE TIGHTLY PACKED HERD.

OOPS!

Feedlot Fiasco

IN AN EFFORT TO SAVE MALDIVA, AG MAN HAS FALLEN BENEATH THE STAMPEDING CATTLE.

OH NO!

AG MAN WORKS HIS WAY UNDER THE COWS, CLINGING WITH HIS VELCRO APPENDAGES.

HE REACHES THE LEAD STEER AND PROPELS HIMSELF OUT IN FRONT OF THE STAMPEDE...

AND WITH A TWIST OF HIS CAP HE BECOMES A STEEL SHARK CAGE SURROUNDING MALDIVA.

GET ME OUTTA THIS FILTHY CAGE OR I'LL SUE!

AG MAN, TRANSFORMED INTO A SHARK CAGE, PROTECTS MALDIVA FROM THE STAMPEDE.

EEEEEEEAAAAAAAAA

MALDIVA IS SAFE BUT LOOKS LIKE A PILE OF BEET-TOP COMPOST.

WITH A TWIST OF HIS CAP, AG MAN FREES MALDIVA FROM THE SHARK CAGE.

BINK

YOU PUTZ! YOU'VE RUINED MY HAIR!

WHAT ABOUT THE DAMAGE YOU'VE DONE TO THE FEEDLOT WITH YOUR PHOSPHORUS HOAX!

IRRELEVANT, MY LITTLE SOIL PRINCESS! AND SO WHAT! IT MADE A GOOD STORY!

MALDIVA, PHOSPHORUS IS ESSENTIAL TO A BALANCED RATION.

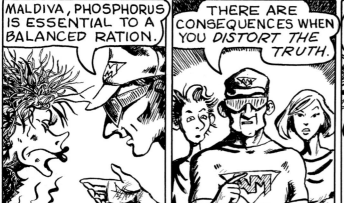

THERE ARE CONSEQUENCES WHEN YOU DISTORT THE TRUTH.

NOT ON TV! HA HA HA HA HA RIGHT, LOR?!

MALDIVA... YOU'RE WARPED. I QUIT!

60 MINUTES HERE I COME!

DEER DEMOLITION

Deer Demolition

YA, WE'RE AVERAGING FIVE *DVA's* A DAY, NOW, RORK.

*DEER VEHICLE ACCIDENTS

WIT ANUDDER TRUCK WE COULD *DOUBLE* OUR TOWS!

YER BRILLIANT, THOR.

LATER THAT DAY...

WHEN I SIGNAL TA CAR IS COMING, YOU LEAD TA DEER 'CROSS TA' ROAD.

JUST LIKE TA PIED PUPAE... YOU KNOW, TA *FLUTE GUY.*

WHAT?

ISN'T THAT PIED PAPAYA?

WE'RE MONITORING THE DEER HERDS BY INFRARED SATELLITE, AG MAN.

BLIP BLIP

WE'VE HAD A DRASTIC RISE IN DEER-VEHICLE ACCIDENTS IN THIS SPECIFIC AREA

BLIP

FEEDING STATION

HWY 37

NORMALLY THEY STAY NEAR THE FEEDING STATION, BUT LATELY WE'VE SEEN THEM RUNNING TO THE HIGHWAY.

YOU MEAN *LIKE THIS?*

GOOD GRIEF!

PROPERTY OF: GREAT LAKES FISH AND GAME

AT FISH & GAME HQ.

LOOK! SOMETHING'S LEADING THE DEER TOWARD THE ROAD!

RADAR

VULTURE TO THOR !!! THE CAR'S *E.T.A.* IS TEN SECONDS. *GO! GO!*

EE EEE

GREAT SCREAMING CERVINE EFFLUVIA! THEY'VE CRASHED!

BLIP BLIP

AT THE SCENE...

YES WE'RE OK. JUST LUCKY THIS TOW TRUCK WAS NEARBY.

SOMETHING'S FISHY...

FISHY? OR *VENISONOID?* MAYBE *THIS* IS A CLUE.

DEER SEASON SALT

20 POUNDS 45.

AHA! I HAVE A PLAN!

VILLAINS BEWARE!

 SHORTLY AFTER DAWN OUR HEROS' PLAN IS ENACTED. AT HQ...

AG MAN! WE'VE GOT DEER ON THE MOVE!

BLIP BLIP

 ROGER!

HEY, I HEAR SOMETHING.

 ANTLERS AT SIX O'CLOCK!

 ROAR

 THE VILLAINOUS THOR AND THE STAMPEDING DEER HAVE TRAMPLED OUR BRAVE CREW.

 A CAR'S COMING! IT'S GOING TO HIT THE DEER!

 THAT'S THOR DRIVING THE DEER. HE RUNS TOW TRUCKS.

 TOWS N' TRUCKS N' DOES N' BUCKS N' LITTLE LAMBS EAT IVY...THIS GUY NEEDS A SERIOUS TALKING TO.

FLIP

?

 AG MAN TRANSFORMS INTO A HENNESSEY, 'VENOM 500'-POWERED DOG SLED

GRAB HOLD!

 REMEMBER THE ALAMO!

 VIVA LAS VEGAS!

 LOOK BEFORE YOU LEEEEPPP

VROOM

EN GARDE, THOR!

 AVAST, MATEYS! YONDER BE THOR!

ROAD HOG!

 ...TIME TO SWITCH FROM PACK-HORSE TO PASSENGER!

 TO THE COUNTY JAIL AND STEP ON IT, MACK!

WHAM

OOF!

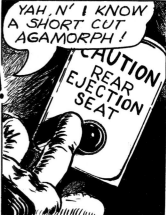 YAH, N' I KNOW A SHORT CUT AGAMORPH!

CAUTION REAR EJECTION SEAT

THOR HAS EJECTED AG MAN INTO THE PATH OF THE DEER.

BUT OUR HERO QUICKLY TRANSFORMS INTO A PIÑATA CONTAINING...

A *FAT-PLUG CRANK-BAIT*, TUNED FOR WINTER AIR.

THE BUCK TOSSES HIS RACK, MAKING A PERFECT CAST.

AG MAN, TRANSFORMED INTO A BASS LURE, SNAGS THOR'S JACKET.

WITH HIS HOOK SET, HE TWISTS HIS CAP AND BECOMES HIMSELF. CAR'S E.T.A. SIX SECONDS!

YER *TOO LATE*, BAGMAN!

BAG MAN?! WHY NOT! WHAT'S HE THINKING?

...AG MAN HAS JUST ONE NANOSECOND BEFORE THE DVA*! *DEER VEHICLE ACCIDENT

HE TRANSFORMS INTO A GIANT *AIRBAG*, INFLATED BEYOND ITS LIMITS AND... K-BLOOEY

STOPS THE DISASTER IN ITS TRACKS

EVERYONE OK? JUST TIDYING UP, FARMBOY.

FISH AND GAME APPRECIATES YOUR HELP, AG MAN

WE HAVE ENOUGH DEER VEHICLE ACCIDENTS WITHOUT THOR MAKING IT WORSE.

WELL, AG MAN, YOU SURE STEPPED ALL OVER THOR'S TOWS.

SHOULDN'T THAT BE *TOES*, FARMBOY.

HOLSTEIN HIJACK

IS THIS THE LOAD WITH THE HEIFER CARRYING THE MICROFILM BOLUS?

YES, THE HEAVY BOLUS WILL REMAIN IN THE RETICULUM INDEFINITELY!

HOW DO THEY GET IT OUT? A RUMENOTOMY, I GUESS

AH... CORN SILK SAN, CUD DIVING!

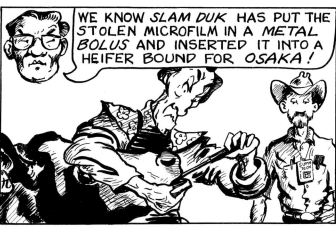

WE KNOW SLAM DUK HAS PUT THE STOLEN MICROFILM IN A METAL BOLUS AND INSERTED IT INTO A HEIFER BOUND FOR OSAKA!

WHAT WAS THAT? A MICROWAVE TRANQUILIZER.

COOL, DUDE. DOES IT PLAY CDs?

SOMEWHERE OVER THE PACIFIC, AG MAN AND CREW HAVE STOWED ABOARD THE VAST

747 CARGO AIRCRAFT CARRYING THE MICRO-FILM DOSED HEIFER AND HER MATES.

SLAM DUK AND HIS NINJAS ARE SURE ATTENTIVE. HEY, FARMBOY!

BE VIGILANT, FARMBOY! OUCH, THIS IS THE LAST TIME I'LL FLY HOLSTEIN CLASS.

SLAM DUK! YOU'RE UNDER ARREST FOR INDUSTRIAL ESPIONAGE!

AG MAN! MY ABLE NEMESIS. YOU HAVE CAUGHT ME!

A QUICK PHOTO, IF I MAY BE PERMITTED?

OH... I GUESS SO. PLEASE TO MOVE A LITTLE LEFT. PLEASE TO SMELL A RAT.

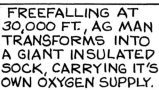

41

TROJAN OSTRICH

Trojan Ostrich

LISTEN TO THIS. "RATITE RUSTLERS ROB RUSTY'S RATITE RANCH!"

REALLY? RHEAS?

NOPE, OSTRICH ABDUCTION.

AND...SOMETHING STRANGE...THERE WERE NO HUMAN FOOTPRINTS!

CORNSILK, ARE YOU THINKING EXTRA-TERRUSTLERS!

HOW'S THE MAAKET, RUDD?

OSTRICH HIDES ARE AT AN ALL-TIME HIGH!

YA! WE COORNA THA MAAKET 'N WE'LL BE RICH!

WE, PEACOCK FACE? GO CHARGE THE DECOY, WE STRIKE AGAIN TONIGHT!

MEANWHILE, BACK AT RUSTY'S RATITE RANCH

AH, THE AGRATOMIC THREE! I'M RUSTY, THANKS FOR COMING!

SO THE RUSTLERS MAKE NO SOUND AND LEAVE NO TRACK?

RIGHT! THE DOGS DON'T EVEN BARK!

RUSTY, FOR THIS STAKEOUT WE'VE BROUGHT OUR OWN DOG. FARMBOY, HEEL!

ARF! ARF!

AG MAN AND FARMBOY DISGUISED AS OSTRICHES ON STAKEOUT

AGRIZAM! LOOK!

CRASH

DUCK! DOWN! BIG BIRD!

DUCK? GOOSE? ERNIE?

WAK!

DUCK!

HE'S LEADING THEM OUT THE GATE!

BOOM!

WHAT'S THAT?

* THE OSTRICH MATING CALL

WHOA!

I THINK WE USED TOO MUCH MAKE-UP.

SIMPLY A NORMAL TERRITORIAL RESPONSE, FARMBOY.

TRANSFORMED INTO AN *APC*, AG MAN AND CREW PURSUE THE OSTRICH NAPPERS.

VAROOM!

ARMORED PERSONNEL CARRIER

THERE THEY ARE!

UDIA INC.

LAAD THE LAST TRUCK AND WE'LL GO!

HALT IN THE NAME OF RATITE RAISERS EVERYWHERE!

CRUNCH

HA! YEW BLASTED AGRIMANIACS CAN'T STOP ME CORNERING THE INTEHNATIONAL OSTRICH HIDE MAAKET!

DON'T COUNT YOUR HIDES BEFORE THEY'RE TANNED, DUD!

YOU TELL'UM, AG MAN.

THAT'S RUDD, AGDUNCE. AND NOW I'LL CEMENT OUR NEW FRIENDSHIP WITH MY HANDY SUPER-GLUE GUN!

CO_2 5 GALLONS

AG MAN QUICKLY TRANSFORMS INTO A DEVICE WHICH GENERATES A WALL OF SYNTHETIC LAMB FAT.

CO_2 5 GALLONS

SPLURT

THE SUPER-GLUE GUN IS NEUTRALIZED.

DRAT!

YIELD, KNAVE! OSTRICH SKIN BOOTS WILL ALWAYS BE AVAILABLE TO THE FREE WORLD!

I AGREE, AGKLUTZ. AVAILABLE...BUT AT MY PRICE!

WAP!

45

Trojan Ostrich

 IN HIS MECHINICAL OSTRICH, RUDD TRYS TO ESCAPE OUR BRAVE AG DEFENDERS

 I'LL GET 'EM! FARMEY, START THE CLOCK

 CORNSILK THROWS A HEEL LOOP.

 GO, SILKY! FIVE FLAT!

 NOT SO FAST, UG MAN! DROP THAT CAP AND KICK IT OVER HERE!

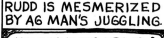

 YOU THINK I NEED SUPERPOWERS TO DEFEAT YOU? WATCH THIS!

 HAND ME THOSE OSTRICH EGGS, FARMBOY.

 AG MAN BEGINS TO JUGGLE OSTRICH EGGS BEFORE THE ASTOUNDED RUSTLER.

 RUDD IS MESMERIZED BY AG MAN'S JUGGLING. INNNCREDIBLE!

 THANKS... YOUR TURN! CLUNK WHUMP BONK

 RUMBLING RATITE! THAT LAST ONE MUST HAVE BEEN HARD BOILED!

 CLOSE... IT WAS FELDSPAR.

 BACK AT RUSTY'S RATITE RANCH H.Q.

THANKS, AG MAN, HERE'S SOME OSTRICH STEAKS TO REMEMBER US BY.

 YOU'RE WELCOME, RUSTY. WE APPRECIATE THE OSTRICH SKIN BOOTS, TOO. RIGHT, CORNSILK?

 RIGHT. BUT RUSTY'S GOT HIS OWN SOUVENIR FROM THE RATITE RUSTLERS

 INDEED! HOW MANY RANCHERS CAN SAY THEY OWN A 500 CALIBER CLOACA.

DINOHYUS REHABITATION PLAN! FARMERS MARCH IN PROTEST!

TERMINATOR PIG

I THOUGHT *DINOHYUS* WAS *EXTINCT*?

COOL! INSTANT ENDANGERED SPECIES!

SAVE COWS

SCALE 1 FT.

DINOHYUS

THEY WERE, FARMY, BUT SCIENTISTS BROUGHT THEM BACK USING *DNA* FRAGMENTS.

Terminator Pig

DINOHYUS HAS BEEN *EXTINCT* FOR NEARLY 20 MILLION YEARS!

AGRITALK FORUM 5

THE GOVERNMENT HAS *NO RIGHT* TO PLACE OUR FARMS AT RISK!

KAGG CH 5

BUT WE OWE THEM LIFE!

THEN RELEASE THEM IN YOUR *OWN* COMMUNITY!

ARE YOU CRAZY! I LIVE NEAR A *PRESCHOOL*!

THANKS FOR COMING, AGRITOMIC THREE. THESE DINOHYUS ARE TEARING UP MY *FARM*.

ROOTING UP MY CROPS, TEARING OUT FENCES AND SHEDS, KILLING CALVES!

LOOK! HERE THEY COME IN BROAD DAYLIGHT!

WHAM!

GRRR

AG MAN TWISTS HIS CAP.

A CHINESE *DRAGON KITE* SHOULD FRIGHTEN THEM AWAY!

TRAMPLE SHRED

WATCH THIS, AG MAN! I'LL SCARE THE HOCKS OFF 'EM!

GOOD WORK, FARMBOY. SHADOW HAMSTERS.

IT'S ALL I KNOW.

THEY'RE COMING BACK!

WITH A TWIST OF HIS CAP, AG MAN TRANSFORMS INTO

BLAST

A BUCK ROGERS MULTI-PASSENGER EJECTION MODULE.

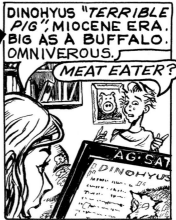

DINOHYUS *"TERRIBLE PIG"*, MIOCENE ERA. BIG AS A BUFFALO. OMNIVEROUS.

MEAT EATER?

MEAT? YEAH, ALONG WITH *POULTRY*, FISH, REDWOODS, AND ALUMINUM SIDING.

AG·SAT

Terminator Pig

FARM BOY'S *HOG CALL* WORKS ON THE *DINOHYUS*...THEY *CHARGE* HIM!

HEY! LOOK AT FARMY! HE JUST *RAN* THE HOG HUNDRED IN 5 FLAT!

AG MAN TRANSFORMS INTO A *BARREL* OF BALER TWINE AND NABS ALL BUT *ONE*!

SKRASH!

THE BIG DINOHYUS BOAR CHASES FARM BOY INTO THE EXHIBIT HALL.

PUFF PANT

THE MAD DINOHYUS CHASES FARM BOY THROUGH THE PLAINS MIOCENE EXHIBIT.

CRASH

SNAP

UH-OH! *TREED*!

HEY! YOU RECYCLED BLT!

SNAP

GRRRR

GRRR EEP?

FLAMING FATBACK! HE'S *DEAD*, FARM BOY!

PLOP

AG MAN! ALL THE DINOHYUS HAVE *DIED*!

MUST BE SOMETHING IN THE ENVIRONMENT THAT WASN'T THERE TWENTY MILLION YEARS AGO.

... BACK AT THE SENATE HEARING.

DINOHYUS WERE FATALLY SENSITIVE TO SYNTHETIC POLYMERS, THAT IS...PLASTIC.

MAYBE REINTRODUCING DISPLACED SPECIES SHOULD BE RECONSIDERED.

HUMANS HAVE ALTERED THE BALANCE OF NATURE. WE CAN'T PRETEND OTHERWISE,

DINOHYUS! WHAT'LL THEY BRING BACK NEXT?

HEY, WAS THAT *ELVIS*?!

YES... AND THEY ARE WILLING TO *KILL* ANIMALS TO SUPPORT THEIR CAUSE *LOOK!*

Better DEAD THAN IN CHAINS

THERE'S STUFF HERE ABOUT MAD COW, FOOT AND MOUTH, TB, BRUCELLOSIS, LYME DISEASE... EVEN *PIN WORMS.*

HAVE THEY *NO IDEA* OF THE CONSEQUENCES OF *BIOTERRORISM?*

CORNSILK, YOU CANNOT REASON WITH A LUNATIC.

MEANWHILE, AT THE ANNUAL ASSOCIATION OF ANIMAL RIGHTS FORCES CONVENTION IN BIG CITY.

FREE SEEING EYE DOGS!

Welcome AARF MEMBERS!

← REGISTRATION

→ MEDIA ROOM

BAN Goldfish Cruelty

FENCE A STEER GO TO JAIL

MINKS AT LAW

DON'T RIDE

NUKE 'em ALL

Neuter Vets NOT Dogs

AARF

LECTURES TODAY

• ATTRACTING AND MAINTAINING REAL CREDIBILITY

• TERRORISM ON THE INTERNET

• MAKING MILLIONS OFF ECOTERRORISM

• RIGHTEOUS INDIGNATION - PULLING IT OFF!

• INSECT SLAVERY - ANT FARM

AND... OUTSIDE THE HOTEL ENTRANCE

END WORLD HUNGER Join 4H

COWBOYS NEED LOVE TOO!

MOSES was Omnivorous

WHILE HIGHER UP, IN A HEAVILY GUARDED ROOM.

WELCOME TO YOU, THE LEADERS, THE ELITE OF AARF. ALLOW ME TO INTRODUCE MR. *SHADE CRAVEN,* MULTI-BILLIONAIRE, MEDIA INTERNET MOGUL, AND C E O OF CRAVEN *MACRO GREEN CONGLOMERATE ENTER-PRISES,* WHO HAS NOW...

TAKEN UP THE ANIMAL RIGHTS CAUSE TO ADD TO HIS LEGACY OF LOOT...UH, THAT IS, HIS LARDER OF LAUD...OR...OR...HIS ACCOMPLISHMENTS! ANYWAY, HERE HE IS! OUR *LEADER! SHADE CRAVEN!*

THANK YOU, BILL, FOR THAT ADEQUATE INTRO-DUCTION. AND NOW... *WELCOME* ...TO... *MY VERSION* OF THE *NEW WORLD!*

YOU ALL KNOW THAT MEMBERSHIP AND FUNDING FOR OUR GROUPS IS IN STEADY DECLINE. WE NEED TO DO *SOMETHING* TO LINE OUR POCKETS AGAIN!

SO WE CAN RID THE WORLD OF *ANIMAL CRUELTY.*

POPPY LANE OF *PDPT* - PRAIRIE DOGS ARE PEOPLE TOO.

OF COURSE, OF COURSE! MANY HAVE TRIED TO ATTRACT ATTENTION TO OUR CAUSE. BUT IT IS HARD TO SHOCK PEOPLE AFTER NINE-ELEVEN.

THROWING PAINT ON PEOPLE, CHASING WHALE BOATS, DRAINING LAKE POWELL, WON'T CUT IT ANYMORE. WHAT I AM ABOUT TO SUGGEST WILL FUND US FOR THE NEXT *FIFTY YEARS!* I PLAN TO THREATEN TO INTRODUCE *FOOT AND MOUTH DISEASE* INTO THE COUNTRY!

WAIT... I DON'T UNDERSTAND. HOW WILL THAT ATTRACT NEW MEMBERS?

IT DOESN'T. THE GOVERNMENT PAYS THE RANSOM.

YES! YES!

I LOVE THIS GUY!

WORLD VENGEANCE ORG. –DOWN WITH FARMING

BUT... WE DON'T REALLY DO IT, RIGHT?

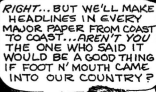

RIGHT...BUT WE'LL MAKE HEADLINES IN EVERY MAJOR PAPER FROM COAST TO COAST...AREN'T YOU THE ONE WHO SAID IT WOULD BE A GOOD THING IF FOOT N' MOUTH CAME INTO OUR COUNTRY?

IT'S TIME TO GET REAL! SOME ANIMALS MAY DIE SO OTHERS CAN BE FREE! DEATH BEFORE SLAVERY!

ALL RIGHT! WE'LL DO IT!

YOU'D ACTUALLY INFECT THE U.S. WITH FOOT AND MOUTH? THAT'S... BIO TERRORISM!

NOT IF THEY MEET OUR DEMANDS. RELEASE ALL ANIMALS IN SERVITUDE. FEEDLOTS, ZOOS, AVIARIES. MEAT EATING IS BANNED! ALL PETS MUST BE RETURNED TO THE WILD...

THAT'S NOT PRACTICAL. BESIDES, WE'D PUT OURSELVES OUT OF BUSINESS.

AS LONG AS WE GET OUR MONEY, WHO CARES.

...I...DON'T KNOW...

POPPY'S PUPPY, HUNK

WOULD A BILLION DOLLARS CHANGE YOUR MIND?

OH, MY GOODNESS! GO ON.

FIRST WE ORGANIZE A GIANT CATTLE DRIVE. SUCK IN ALL THE COWBOY TYPES, JOHN WAYNE WANNABEES. LET 'EM JOIN THE RIDE TO PARTICIPATE. WE CALL IT THE CATTLE DRIVE FOR CANCER, OR HEART DISEASE, OR SCURVY, WHO CARES BECAUSE IT'S JUST A FRONT ANYWAY.

WE GET SCHOOL KIDS AROUND THE COUNTRY TO SPONSOR STEERS, THEY COLLECT MONEY DOOR TO DOOR TO BE A PART. WE ATTRACT NATIONAL SPONSORS. IT WILL WORK! PEOPLE ARE SUCH SUCKERS.

THIS IS GREAT! WE CAN SHUT DOWN AGRICULTURE!

NO MORE CHEMICALS!

NO MORE WOODEN HOUSES. ONLY CINDER BLOCK OR ADOBE!

NO MORE PROFITS TO BE MADE OFF THE BACKS OF INNOCENT ANIMALS!

BACK TO THE ORGANIC LIFESTYLE!

OREGANO OREGANO UNH UNH UNH!

DOWN WITH

THE DEMANDS SEEM SO EXTREME. PEOPLE WILL NOT WANT TO GIVE UP THEIR PETS

I AGREE

LEW WARD OF THE ANIMAL RIGHTS FUND RAISERS ASSN.

OUR MEMBERS WILL DESERT US. MAYBE ONLY CERTAIN PEOPLE COULD OWN PETS.

RIGHT! ONLY CERTAIN PETS DOGS AND CATS. NO HORSES OR RODENTS OR GOD FORBID... DAIRY COWS, THAT'S TOO BIG A LOOPHOLE FARMERS COULD CLAIM THE DAIRY COWS WERE PETS!

THAT WOULD WORK.

WE COULD STILL AIM OUR FUNDRAISING TOWARD THE KINDNESS ANGLE, AND CRUELTY.

DEAR ME. YOU STILL DON'T GET IT. THERE WILL BE NO REASON TO RAISE FUNDS

THEN...WHAT WILL WE DO?

YOU CAN GIVE EVERYONE ON YOUR STAFF A MILLION BUCKS AND DONATE YOUR BUILDING TO THE UNEMPLOYED FARMER'S ASSOCIATION!

HA HA HA

BUT, WHAT IF THERE ARE STILL INJURED ANIMALS, DOGS HIT BY CARS BIRDS WITH BROKEN WINGS, CATS HAVING TROUBLE QUEENING?

IN THE NEW WORLD ANIMALS ARE FREE. ON THEIR OWN, JUST LIKE IN THE JUNGLE. PRACTICING VETERINARY MEDICINE WILL BE ILLEGAL

PEOPLE WILL LIVE WITHIN THE CITY LIMITS ANIMALS WILL ROAM AT WILL.

BUT...

AHH, I GET IT. YOU WANT MORE THAN MONEY, YOU WANT POWER! OK, START YOUR OWN ANIMAL RIGHTS POLICE! I'LL PUT IT IN THE DEMANDS.

Typhoid Mary Trail Drive

THANK YOU... NOW THAT I HAVE YOUR ATTENTION...

FLID...

THIS IS NOT THE WAY TO MAKE OUR POINT. WE LIVE IN A *FREE COUNTRY*. DESTROYING PROPERTY OR PREVENTING FREEDOM OF SPEECH IS AGAINST THE LAW. NO MATTER HOW LOONY, MISGUIDED OR EVIL. IF THE ACTIVISTS BREAK THE LAW, THEY *WILL* BE PUNISHED!

ARF MEDIA ROOM

GOT MILK?

Free BBQ

GATHER UP YOUR STUFF, AND LEAVE QUIETLY.

WE BETTER INVITE *HIM* ALONG. BE A GOOD WAY TO KEEP AN EYE ON 'EM.

PARDON ME, AREN'T YOU *SHADE CRAVEN, CEO* OF CRAVEN MACROGREEN CONGLOMERATED ENTERPRISES?

NO M'AM, YOU MUST BE MISTAKEN.

...BUT, I JUST WANTED TO—

SAVE IT, SISTER

WELL... OKAY

SPLOOK

CARE FOR SOME RHUBARB PIE?

AND SO... AG MAN, CORNSILK AND, FARMBOY FIND THEMSELVES SADDLED UP FOR WHAT THEY THINK WILL BE THE *CATTLE DRIVE FOR CANCER.*

THAT'S ROWDY BATES, UP AHEAD, THE TRAIL BOSS.

YES. HE WORKED FOR THE *ROCKING A.* A GOOD COW MAN.

WHO'S THAT?

...DON'T KNOW. BUT HE LOOKS *STEREOTYPICAL.*

YOU READY FOR THIS, TWEEZER?

58

CORNSILK AND ROWDY ARE RACING TO TURN THE LEAD STEER.

AG MAN TWISTS HIS CAP, WONDERING WHAT TO BECOME.

POPPY LANE *TRIPS*.

HELP ME!

AT FULL GALLOP, CORNSILK LEANS IN FOR POPPY.

AG MAN, MAKING UP HIS MIND, TRANSFORMS INTO A GIANT ARCADE CRANE.

SPROING

WHOA, DUDE.

CORNSILK NABS POPPY...

AAAHHHHHH

AND AG MAN SNATCHES BOTH UP AND ABOVE THE RAMPAGING STEERS.

ROWDY TURNS THE STAMPEDE FROM THE PROTESTERS.

WOW! DID YOU SEE THAT.!?

YUP, AG MAN IS IMPRESSIVE.

NOOOOOOOO. I MEAN THE *SUPER CHICK*, CORNSYRUP. ... WONDER IF I COULD *PROGRAM HER*?!

ARE YOU ALL RIGHT?

IT *NEVER* WOULD HAVE HAPPENED IF YOU HADN'T STARTED THIS *STUPID TRAILDRIVE*!

YOU'RE WELCOME.

IT'S ALL YOUR FAULT!

AT LEAST YOU'RE NOT HURT, I'LL CHECK THE OTHERS.

YUP, JUST YOUR EVERYDAY TECHNO FREAK GEEK WITH HIS *HANDS ON THE WHEEL.*

HA! THAT'S GOOD! BUT NEXT TIME YOU *ASK FIRST.*

MAYBE...

NO *MAYBES* ABOUT IT.

BACK IN THE AG TENT.

ISN'T IT ODD...

THAT THE STEERS HAVE DISPLAYED ABNORMAL BEHAVIOR *TWICE.*

COULD BE COINCIDENCE BUT...

ONE OF MY OLD PROFS USED TO SAY "TWO'S COINCIDENCE, THREE'S AN EPIDEMIC."

FARMY, I SAW YOU TALKING WITH THE ANIMAL RIGHTS PROTESTOR LADY.

I JUST INVITED HER INTO CAMP, OFFERED HER SOME SUPPER.

YOU'RE SO NAÏVE. DON'T LET HER SUCKER YOU IN.

CORNSILK'S RIGHT, FARMBOY. ERR ON THE SIDE OF CAUTION. THESE ARE PEOPLE CAPABLE OF BIOTERRORISM. THEY BOMB LABORATORIES AND BURN SKI RESORTS. MANY WOULD SPIKE YOU AS QUICK AS THEY WOULD SPIKE A TREE.

NIGHT FARMBOY

NIGHT AG MAN

NIGHT CORNSILK

DAY 30 · DOWN TO FIFTEEN STEERS

JUNE

65

On the Trail

CHUCK WAGON

HEY, IS THAT GPS?

HUH? OH, I GUESS IT COULD BE... I CALL IT A *SUPERPALM.*

COULD I TAKE A LOOK?

NO!

...I MEAN, I'D RATHER NOT...IT'S SORT OF MY INVENTION.

I UNDERSTAND. I'D FEEL THAT WAY TOO. YOU DESIGN SOFTWARE?

OH YEAH, SOFT, HARD, *THIS BABY IS A MULTI-PLANE MANIPULATOR.*

WHAT CAN IT DO?

CALCS, GLOBAL SYSTEMS AWARENESS, ALL THE USUAL, PLUS, IT TRANSMITS COMMANDS TO *DRONE RECEIVERS!*

DRONE RECEIVERS?

LIKE, IF I'M *NOT* HOME, I CAN *FEED THE DOG,* TURN ON THE LIGHTS, WATER THE YARD.

DOG CHOW

BUZZT

FLIP

PC

SLINK

COOL

I CAN EVEN MAKE MY DOG DO TRICKS. LIKE, I HAVE A DRONE RECEIVER ON HIS COLLAR THAT TRANSMITS ELECTRICAL IMPULSES TO HIS BRAIN! IF I, LIKE, WANT HIM TO ROLL OVER, I PUNCH IN THE CODE ON MY REMOTE AND... *SEND.*

REVO-COO-LUTIONARY! AND YOU CAN DO IT FROM *ANYWHERE* VIA SATELLITE!

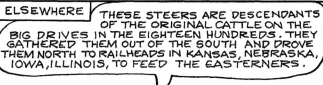

I SAW YOUR TIRE WAS FLAT, YOU'VE LOST TEN POUNDS SINCE WE STARTED, YOUR SNEAKERS ARE FLAPPING, YOU'RE ALWAYS ANGRY, YOU'VE YET TO SAY A KIND WORD. YOU SEEM PRETTY FRUSTRATED. I'M SURE IT'S NOT EASY.

NOT EASY! EVERY-ONE THINKS I'M A LUNATIC, NINETY-SIX PERCENT OF THE PEOPLE EAT MEAT. SINCE NINE-ELEVEN NOBODY TAKES US SERIOUSLY. I'M PUSHING A BUSTED BIKE, FOLLOWING HAPPY PEOPLE DRIVING COWS... STEERS, TO THEIR DEATHS. I'M LIVING ON CANDY BARS AND TOFU AND GELATIN. NO! IT'S NOT EASY, AND IT DOESN'T HELP FOR YOU AND YOUR AGRICULTURAL ROBOTS TO KEEP CHECKING ON MY HEALTH! SO, BUTT OUT!

I'LL JUST SAY THIS. PERSONALLY, I DON'T LIKE YOU, BUT I DON'T KNOW IF YOU ACT LIKE A CLOACA ALL THE TIME OR IF IT'S JUST FOR US. BUT... WHAT IS IT WITH US PEOPLE? WHEN YOU SPEND YOUR LIFE AROUND ANIMALS, CARING FOR THEM, RIDING, EATING, TRAIN-ING THEM, YOU GET IN A DIFFERENT RHYTHM THAN FOLKS WHO EXIST ONLY AMONGST THEIR OWN SPECIES. IN OUR CASE, WE SHARE OUR SPACE WITH ANIMALS. WE RESPECT THEIR PLACE ON EARTH AND IN THE FOOD CHAIN. IN YOUR WORLD, YOU ARE LIKE FISH IN THE SEA ALWAYS ON THE LOOKOUT FOR SMALLER FISH TO EAT OR BIGGER FISH THAT MIGHT EAT YOU. YOUR GUIDING PRINCIPLE IS SAFETY IN NUMBERS. ALWAYS HOPING THE ONE NEXT TO YOU WILL BE EATEN. IN OUR WORLD, THERE IS ROOM FOR KINDNESS, BECAUSE WE HAVE LEARNED TO ACCOMODATE FOR THE HABITS OF SPECIES OTHER THAN OUR OWN. SO, MAYBE THAT'S WHY EVERY NOW AND THEN SOMEBODY SAYS, "HOW'S THE ANIMAL RIGHTS LUNATIC DOIN'?" YOU CAN BET IT'S NOT BECAUSE YOU ARE SO POPULAR AND PLEASANT TO BE AROUND. YOU BETTER PUT ON SOME SUN SCREEN. YOU LOOK LIKE A BOILED SHRIMP. BY THE WAY, GELATIN, COMES FROM THE BONES, CARTILAGE AND TENDONS OF COWS.

THEY APPROACH A PRISTINE MOUNTAIN LAKE.

BOYS, EASE 'EM UP FOR A DRINK OF WATER.

OK, GIZMO GEEK, YOU'RE ON. SHOW ME SOME BAYWATCH.

HEY! IT WOULD REALLY BE COOL IF WE COULD OUTFIT THE STEERS IN SPEEDOS.

EHHHHH, FERGET IT. JUST TAKE 'M FER A SWIM.

YOU'VE ACTUALLY DONE WELL, ROWDY, BUT *I'M PUZZLED* BY THE BEHAVIOR OF THE STEERS.

WE'VE HAD SEVERAL BIZARRE INSTANCES, AS FARMBOY PROBABLY TOLD YOU. YESTERDAY THEY TRAVELED IN A *VEE*, LIKE A SKEIN OF GEESE...ALL DAY.

THEY'VE CIRCLED LIKE MUSK OXEN.

LEAPED LIKE SALMON GOING UP A LADDER.

YEP, THERE'S SOMETHING FISHY GOING ON HERE.

...BAD

MAYBE I BETTER STAY FOR THE DURATION OF THE RIDE.

MUCH OBLIGED, AG MAN, MUCH OBLIGED

CORNSILK KEEPS HER AG-TV AUDIENCE INFORMED WITH THE GENEROUS HELP OF STATIONS IN TOWNS ALONG THE TRAIL.

KFRM

THANKS FOR THE AIR TIME, RUSTY.

YOU'RE WELCOME ANYTIME, CORNSILK.

WHEAT, CORN, AND SOYBEANS HOLDING STEADY AT ROCK BOTTOM. AND THAT'S THE *MARKET.* NOW FOR THE LATEST ON THE CRAVEN MACRO-GREEN CHARITY TRAIL DRIVE.

ACCORDING TO ROWDY BATES, TRAIL BOSS, TEN STEERS REMAIN AS THEY CROSS THE HIGH DESERT COUNTRY. TWENTY-NINE HAVE BEEN LEFT ALONG THE CROSS-COUNTRY ROUTE AS *GOODWILL AMBASSADORS* FOR AGRICULTURE.

Typhoid Mary Trail Drive

SURPRISE, AG BUNGLER! NOW, STEP BACK BEFORE YOU GET HURT!

WHAT ARE YOU DOING?!

GIVE ME MY CAP, CRAVEN.

YOU WANT A CAP?

ZING

OLE!

TRY THIS ON FOR SIZE!

WHAP!

CRAVEN CHANGES HIS ARM INTO A SKILLET.

UHH

NOW! HAVE I GOT YOUR ATTENTION?! IS EVERYBODY AWAKE?! I HAVE IN MY HAND A REMOTE CONTROL THAT CAN ACTIVATE..

THIRTY SATELLITE-LINKED IMPLANTS THAT CAN UNLEASH DEATH AND DESTRUCTION ALL ACROSS THE COUNTRY.

EACH STEER WE LEFT ALONG THE WAY ON THIS TYPHOID MARY TRAIL DRIVE IS IMPLANTED WITH A CAPSULE CONTAINING LIVE FOOT AND MOUTH VIRUS. ONE PUSH OF THE REMOTE WILL RUPTURE THE IMPLANT AND INFECT THE BEAST

ZAP

POP

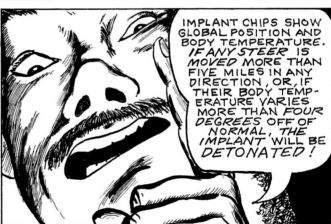

IMPLANT CHIPS SHOW GLOBAL POSITION AND BODY TEMPERATURE. IF ANY STEER IS MOVED MORE THAN FIVE MILES IN ANY DIRECTION, OR, IF THEIR BODY TEMPERATURE VARIES MORE THAN FOUR DEGREES OFF OF NORMAL, THE IMPLANT WILL BE DETONATED!

FOOT AND MOUTH WILL SPREAD LIKE WILDFIRE!

BUT... WHY?

RIPP PP!

AARF

GASP

THIS IS A NEW DAY FOR ENSLAVED ANIMALS EVERYWHERE!

AARF

BUT SO MANY ANIMALS WILL *SUFFER* IF YOU DO THIS!

BETTER *DEATH* THAN SLAVERY! SOME MUST BE SACRIFICED!

BUT...

ENOUGH! YOU AG FOOLS, COW PROVOKERS AND PIG PLANTATION PLUNDERERS! IF YOU MEET OUR DEMANDS WE WILL *NOT* RELEASE THE CONTAGION.

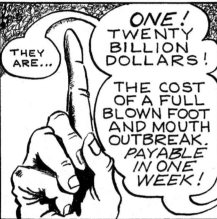

THEY ARE...

ONE! TWENTY BILLION DOLLARS! THE COST OF A FULL BLOWN FOOT AND MOUTH OUTBREAK. *PAYABLE IN ONE WEEK!*

TWO! AN IMMEDIATE END TO EATING *MEAT!* FROM KRILL TO KANGAROO, FROM FISH EGGS TO FILET MIGNON!

THREE! THE RELEASE OF ALL ANIMALS IN DOMESTIC CAPTIVITY FROM GOLDFISH TO CATS, HAMSTERS TO HORSES, COCKATOOS TO COWS!

I'M INVITING A MEMBER OF THE AG MAN TEAM TO JOIN ME DURING THE TRANSITION.

HEY!

IF YOU NEED A *HOSTAGE*, YOU CRAVEN COWARD, TAKE ME!

TAKE A HIKE, YOU CAPLESS NON-ACTION CARTOON BUFFOON!

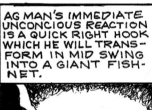

AG MAN'S IMMEDIATE UNCONCIOUS REACTION IS A QUICK RIGHT HOOK WHICH HE WILL TRANSFORM IN MID SWING INTO A GIANT FISH-NET.

BUT, THEN HIS BRAIN CATCHES UP.

OOPS

TWISTING THE STOLEN CAP, SHADE CRAVEN TRANSFORMS INTO A HARP.

PING

AHHHHHH

SPROING!

JUST DO AS YOU'RE TOLD, AG BUM, AND SHE'LL BE RETURNED UNHARMED.

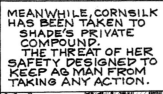

I'VE HAD SOME TIME TO REFLECT. I'VE NOT CHANGED MY MIND ABOUT ANIMAL RIGHTS. THEY SHOULD BE TREATED LIKE...I ALMOST SAID *PEOPLE*, BUT I DON'T BELIEVE THAT. THEY JUST *SHOULDN'T BE EXPLOITED* AND *RAISED FOR PROFIT!*

THE WORLD WOULD BE BETTER OFF IF NOBODY ATE MEAT.

I'VE HEARD ALL THIS BEFORE. YOU CAN LEAVE.

NO, *PLEASE*, LET ME FINISH. I'VE GOT A NEW UNDERSTANDING OF LIVESTOCK PEOPLE. I'VE NEVER BEEN AROUND YOUR KIND.

YES, WE'RE SO MUCH MORE SINISTER THAN SHADE CRAVEN AND HIS BUNCH OF TERRORISTS.

I AM REPELLED BY SHADE CRAVEN!

BUT NOT BY THE MONEY. WHAT'S YOUR CUT, A BILLION?

UNFORTUNATELY, IT HAS ALL BECOME "ABOUT THE MONEY" AND *NOT ABOUT THE ANIMALS.*

SAVE THE ZOPILOTE

GIVE

YOU ARE A WEAKLING. YOU'RE WILLING TO LET THAT *MADMAN* THREATEN THE *WELL BEING* OF A *NATION*, TO LET HIM *UNLEASH* UNIMAGINABLE *SUFFERING* ON ANIMALS YOU DON'T LIKE, *AND...* WHETHER YOU *LIKE* IT OR *NOT*, INCREASE THE COST OF FOOD TO *EVERYONE*.

AND *WHY*? GREED. MAYBE IT'S TIME YOU *LEFT* BEFORE I SAY SOMETHING I'LL REGRET.

I KNOW SOMETHING YOU DON'T. SHADE PLANS TO *RELEASE* THE FOOT AND MOUTH VIRUS AS *SOON* AS HE GETS THE MONEY, *PERIOD!*

HE COULD CARE LESS ABOUT THE WELFARE OF THE PLANET. I CANNOT *BE A PARTY* TO HIS *TREACHERY*. HE MUST *BE STOPPED!* BUT I DON'T KNOW HOW.

DID I HEAR YOU RIGHT?

YES.

WE HAVE FOUR DAYS TILL THE RANSOM IS DUE. IF YOU CAN GET ME A COMPUTER, I CAN CONTACT AG MAN. HE'S PROBABLY WORKING ON A PLAN NOW.

TWO HOURS LATER

BY THE WAY, I'M GETTING AWFULLY TIRED OF WASHING OUT THESE CLOTHES EVERY NIGHT IN THE SINK

SORRY. I'LL FIND YOU SOMETHING.

AG MAN SAYS THEY MUST DETERMINE IF THE THREAT IS A HOAX, OR, IF THE VIRUS IS *REAL*.

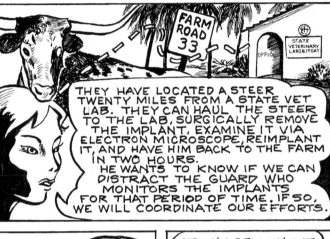

FARM ROAD 33

OFFICE

STATE VETERINARY LABORATORY

THEY HAVE LOCATED A STEER TWENTY MILES FROM A STATE VET LAB. THEY CAN HAUL THE STEER TO THE LAB, SURGICALLY REMOVE THE IMPLANT, EXAMINE IT VIA ELECTRON MICROSCOPE, REIMPLANT IT, AND HAVE HIM BACK TO THE FARM IN TWO HOURS.
HE WANTS TO KNOW IF WE CAN *DISTRACT* THE GUARD WHO MONITORS THE IMPLANTS FOR THAT PERIOD OF TIME. IF SO, WE WILL COORDINATE OUR EFFORTS.

TELL AG MAN WE WILL BE READY TOMORROW AT MIDNIGHT AND GIVE HIM *TWO FULL HOURS*.

HOW?

I KNOW WHO IS GUARD THAT SHIFT...TWEEZER, AND, COINCIDENTALLY, HE TOLD ME HE'D LIKE TO KNOW YOU BETTER.

TWEEZER?! YOU WOULDN'T *DARE* DO *THAT* TO ME.

HEY, I'M SELLIN' OUT HERE. YOU CAN AT LEAST DO A LITTLE DIVERSIONARY *HAND TO HAND* COMBAT.

WHAT DO YOU HAVE IN MIND?

I'LL ARRANGE A MIDNIGHT *DINNER DATE*. THEN, I VOLUNTEER TO MONITOR THE IMPLANTS WHILE YOU'RE DINING. IT WOULD JUST BE OUR *LITTLE SECRET*.

TELL THE LITTLE WEASEL THAT FLOWERS WOULD BE NICE.

MIDNIGHT, THE NEXT NIGHT

KNOCK KNOCK

LET'S GET THIS GUY LOADED, AG MAN. TWO HOURS DOESN'T GIVE US MUCH TIME.

COME IN, TWEEZER.

MEANWHILE...

IT'S MIDNIGHT, DOC, FARMBOY, LET'S ROLL

SLAM!

DON'T WORRY ABOUT A THING, TWEEZE. I'LL BE EXPECTING YOU AT TWO AM SHARP. HAVE FUN, YOU TWO!

COME SIT AT THE TABLE. POPPY ORDERED US *TAKE OUT*. SORRY IT'S NOT FANCIER. BUT, SHE'S A VEGETARIAN, YA KNOW. WOULD YOU LIKE A NATURAL FRUIT DRINK?

UH, HERE'S SOME FLOWERS... THEY'RE PLASTIC

IT'S VERY THOUGHTFUL OF YOU, TWEEZER. IS THAT YOUR *REAL NAME*?

IT'S SHORT FOR *TWEEZERISHUS*. IS CORNSILK YOUR REAL NAME?

YES. I HAVE A SISTER NAMED *DANDY LION*, AND A BROTHER NAMED *BOBBOKRA*.

PRETTY SLICK OUT THERE. WISH THESE WIPERS WERE FASTER.

WITH A TWIST OF HIS CAP, (YES, TROOPS, HE HAD A SPARE.) AG MAN'S ARM BECOMES A WINDSHIELD WIPER.

THAT'S BETTER

JUST HOLD HER STEADY, DOC. IT'S TEN AFTER. I TOLD THE LAB WE'D BE THERE BY TWELVE-THIRTY.

SO, HOW *DID* YOU GET SO SMART?

I'VE ALWAYS BEEN *BRILLIANT*. WHEN I WAS *TWO*, I REWIRED DAD'S *TV* REMOTE TO OPEN AND CLOSE THE GARAGE. BY FIRST GRADE I WAS MAKING EXPLODING EASTER EGGS, BIRD DECOYS THAT SHOCKED CATS, DOG COLLARS THAT MADE THEM VOMIT. THEN, WHEN I GOT TO *MIDDLE SCHOOL*, I...

THE VETERINARY DIAGNOSTIC LABORATORY, TWELVE THIRTY-ONE, AM.

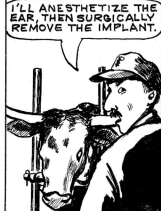

I'LL ANESTHETIZE THE EAR, THEN SURGICALLY REMOVE THE IMPLANT.

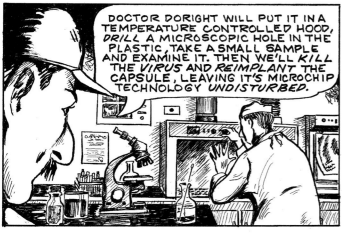

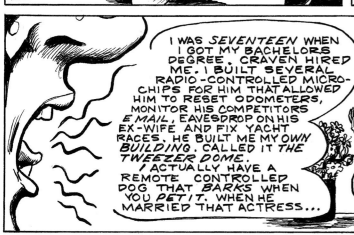

EVERYTHING GOOD WITH YOU?

WHAT CAN I SAY? SHE *LOVES* ME.

WITH THE HELP OF POPPY, CORNSILK IS ABLE TO CONTACT FARMBOY WITH INFORMATION ABOUT THE REMOTE CONTROL SATELLITE TRANSMISSION DEVICE THAT ACTIVATES THE IMPLANT THAT RELEASES THE *FOOT* AND *MOUTH* VIRUS INTO THE BLOOD STREAM OF THE IMPLANTED STEERS.
FARM BOY LOCATES THE SATELLITE, AND WITH AG MAN TRANSFORMED INTO A SPACEFIGHTER, THEY HUNT IT DOWN AND REMOVE THE ANTENNA A MERE TWO HOURS BEFORE CRAVEN'S DEADLINE.

THE FOLLOWING DAY, AT THE COMPOUND.

MISTER CRAVEN!

I'VE LOST CONTACT WITH THE SATELLITE!

WHAT?!

HOW COULD THAT HAPPEN?!

I DON'T KNOW. *I SWEAR* OUR SATELLITE COORDINATES WERE *TOP SECRET*. AND, OUR EQUIPMENT *HERE* IS WORKING FINE.

IT'S POSSIBLE THAT *SPACE DEBRIS* COULD HAVE *HIT* THE SATELLITE, DAMAGING IT.

WHAM

DON'T BREATHE A *WORD* OF THIS TO *ANYONE!* IN LESS THAN AN HOUR THE *DEPARTMENT OF AGRICULTURE* WILL BE WIRING *TWENTY BILLION DOLLARS* TO MY *SECRET BANK ACCOUNT. NO ONE WILL BE THE WISER. AND, DON'T FORGET,* I'VE *STILL* GOT *CORNSILK* AS A *BARGAINING CHIP!*

CORNSILK! ...SAY, COULD I BORROW THIS? NOW SHE'LL *REALLY* BE IMPRESSED!

CHECK THIS, BABE.

BING

GIVE ME THAT!

WHOA. I GUESS IT TAKES A LITTLE PRACTICE.

BART, MEET ME OUT BACK WITH THE GIRL. I WANT HER WHERE I CAN SEE HER TILL THE MONEY TRANSFERS.

ROGER BOSS

SOON. ENJOY THE FRESH AIR, MY DEAR. AS SOON AS THOSE AG FOOLS PAY UP, THE MONEY WILL BE SCATTERED TO SECRET ACCOUNTS WORLD-WIDE AND YOU'LL BE FREE TO GO. BUT, I BELIEVE I'LL KEEP THE CAP.

THAT MIGHT NOT BE SO EASY.

AT CRAVEN'S NOT-SO-SECRET HIDEOUT.

CRAVEN!

WHA...

I'VE GOT BAD CULINARY NEWS FOR YOU, SHADE. YOUR GOOSE IS COOKED.

A HOLLOW THREAT AGROPITHICUS IGNORAMUS, CONSIDERING I'M THE ONE WITH THE CAP AND THE GIRL, AND YOU'RE THE ONE WITH THE GOOFY WAYFARERS.

NOW YOU'VE DONE IT CRAVEN. THOSE GLASSES WERE HIS FATHER'S, AG MAN SENIOR.

HA HA HA!

UH. BOSS.

WHAT!

HE'S...HE'S GOT A...

OH... DID I FORGET TO MENTION, I HAVE A SPARE.

YOU'RE LYING! IT'S A FAKE!

AG MAN TWISTS HIS CAP.

A FAKE?! YOU COULD BE RIGHT! I BETTER CHECK IT OUT. ROUND BALER!

BING

PERPETUAL MOTION MACHINE.

BING

TACK ROOM CLEANING DEVICE.

BING

MECHANICAL DAIRYMAN.

BING

ANY QUESTIONS?

CRAVEN TRANSFORMS HIS HAND INTO A ROCK.

BOINK

WHAT DO *YOU* SAY BART?... *BART!* UMM, OUT LIKE A MACKEREL.

OH *GOOD!* THE HUMAN FRECKLE, GOD'S GIFT TO THE *BAD PUN,* IS *HERE.* I'LL BE ABLE TO GET RID OF *ALL* OF YOU AT ONCE!

ON YOUR MARKS...

SHADE CRAVEN, A BLACK BELT IN EVIL, TRANSFORMS INTO A SUBURBAN WITH A SMALL BLOCK CHEVY 410" INJECTED MOTOR AND A *CUSTOM KILLER GRILLE GUARD.*

GO!

VROOM

EQUIPTED WITH *Craven Stru*

AG MAN HAS ONLY A MOMENT TO REACT.

HE GRABS HIS CAP, AND TRUE TO FORM, MORPHS INTO A STONE POST FROM KANSAS.

KA RASH

CRAVEN, IN A BLINDING RAGE, SPINS HIS CAP AND BECOMES A GIANT ROBOT-VINEGAROON, HIS ABDOMEN LOADED WITH *HYDROCHLORIC ACID!*

HISSSSSSSSS

$2HCl + CaCO_3$

$= CaCl_2 + H_2CO_3$

$H_2CO_3 = H_2O + CO_2$

AG MAN STEELS HIMSELF AGAINST THE PAIN AND FORCES HIMSELF TO MAKE A LAST DESPERATE TRANSFORMATION...

AND CRAVEN SUDDENLY FINDS HIMSELF IMMOBILIZED IN LUCITE.

HEY! I USED TO HAVE A PAPERWEIGHT LIKE THAT.

AG MAN BELCHES OUT THE STOLEN CAP.

I GOT IT!

SPLORP

AND BOTH TRANSFORM BACK INTO HUMAN FORM.

BING BING

HEY... MY... MY...

I BELIEVE THAT'S GAME, SET, AND CAP!

CORNSILK WRAPS UP THE TALE OF THE TRAIL DRIVE FOR HER AG NEWS AUDIENCE.

SHADE CRAVEN WAS EXPOSED TODAY FOR WHAT HE REALLY IS, A COMPLETE FRAUD, AN EVIL MANIPULATOR WHO WILL USE THE GULLIBLE AND CON THE WEAK TO ADVANCE HIS POSITION IN THE WORLD OF POWER AND COMMERCE.

COURTROOM FOOTAGE COURTESY CH 7

ANTI GROUPS, IN AN EFFORT TO ESTABLISH SOME CREDIBILITY IN THE WAKE OF THEIR COMPLICITY IN CRAVEN'S BIO-TERRORIST ATTACK, ARE RETHINKING THEIR POSITIONS ON ANIMAL RIGHTS, ENVIRONMENT, AND BASIC HUMAN RESPONSIBILITY TO EACH OTHER.

MEANWHILE, BACK IN THE COUNTRY, WHEAT IS STABLE, PORK-BELLIES ARE UP AND WE NEED RAIN. THIS IS CORN SILK, YOUR AG NEWS REPORTER REMINDING YOU...

TO PLANT SOMETHING TODAY. A SEED, A KIND WORD, OR AN IDEA.

AFTER THE BROADCAST.

ANOTHER GOOD JOB, CORNSILK, SO, WHAT HAPPENED TO SHADE CRAVEN AND HIS IGNOMINIOUS CREW?

INDICTMENTS CHARGING BIO-TERRORISM ARE FILED AGAINST CRAVEN, BLACK BART, TWEEZER, AND POPPY.

POPPY, TOO, HUH?

I'M TESTIFYING ON HER BEHALF, WITHOUT HER WE'D HAVE HAD A DISASTER OF HISTORIC PROPORTIONS. WE'VE GAINED A MUTUAL RESPECT. BUT SHE'S PROBABLY GOING TO JAIL.

YES, IT'S A SHAME. WELL, HERE WE ARE AT YOUR PLACE. SAY, ISN'T THAT ROWDY'S RIG?

IT IS. I TOLD HIM I'D GIVE HIS DAUGHTER SOME TIPS ON BARREL RACING.

SO, WHAT D'YA WANNA DO, AG MAN?

OH, I DON'T KNOW. HAVE YOU EVER SEEN ARIZONA?

UM... ON THE MAP HERE IT'S YELLOW.

ABOUT THE AUTHOR AND ARTIST

Brothers Baxter and Bob Black were raised in Las Cruces, New Mexico and were active in 4-H and FFA.

Baxter has written many books of ag humor and cowboy poetry. Bob has illustrated many of them. It is a nice arrangement since neither has a steady job. They call it being 'self-unemployed.' Baxter practiced veterinary medicine for several years and now makes a living being humorous. He has a few cows. Bob is a Vietnam vet, former postal worker and today is a full-time artist.

Both live in Arizona and each is married with children. They have two other brothers who have real jobs and they all call their mother every Sunday.

Baxter Black

Bob Black

MORE OF BAXTER'S STUFF

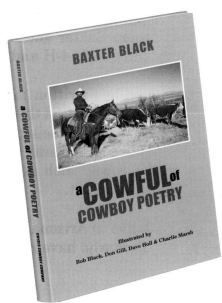

BOOKS

COYOTE COWBOY POETRY © 1986
CROUTONS ON A COW PIE, VOL 2 © 1992
HEY, COWBOY, WANNA GET LUCKY?
    (Penguin Putnam) © 1995
CACTUS TRACKS & COWBOY PHILOSOPHY
    (Crown Publishing) © 1997
A COWFUL OF COWBOY POETRY © 2000
HORSESHOES, COWSOCKS & DUCKFEET
    (Crown Publishing, Inc.) © 2003

VIDEO TAPES

BAXTER BLACK'S FIRST VIDEO
BAXTER BLACK BY HIMSELF
BAXTER BLACK RIDIN' HIGH

CD's

BAXTER BLACK'S DOUBLE CD
COWBOY MENTALITY PLUS
THE BIG ONE THAT GOT AWAY BLUES (2 CD's)

If you can't find any of these items at your local bookstore,
check your local co-op, veterinarian, feed store, western
wear store or give us a call . . . (800) 654-2550.
www.baxterblack.com